Watch Out, Nebit!

Written by Katie Dale

Illustrated by Aleksandar Zolotić

Collins

My little dog Nebit is my best friend.

We go everywhere together ...

most of the time.

"Oh no! Watch out, Nebit!"

3

Nebit runs across the crowded street.

The muck spreaders are smearing stinky dung around the houses to keep the rats away.

But where is little Nebit?

Oh no! He's kicked over the mucky bucket.

"Watch out, Nebit!"

Oh no! Nebit scurries into an opulent house.

The chef is cooking antelope for dinner.

Nebit scuttles into the bathroom.

How strange! Someone is filling the bath with milk to make their skin soft.

But where is little Nebit?

Oh no! He's spilt all the milk.

"Watch out, Nebit!"

Don't cry over spilt milk!

9

Nebit sprints to the river.

Fishermen are catching slippery fish for their dinner.

But where is little Nebit?

Oh no! The fisherman is fuming. He has lost all his fish.

"Watch out, Nebit!"

Nebit bounds onto the boats.

One barge is even decorated with fragrant flowers — maybe the queen is inside!

But where is little Nebit?

Oh no! He's nudged the girl's ladder.

"Watch out, Nebit!"

Nebit leaps over the stepping stones …

But help! They're not *stones*, after all!

Snap!

14

15

Nebit escapes into the desert.

The giant sphinx glares at me as I pass.

But where is little Nebit?

Oh no! Don't wake the grumpy camels.

"Watch out, Nebit!"

Nebit disappears down a shadowy tunnel.

There are drawings on the wall that tell a story.

Nebit?

But where is Nebit?

How will I find him in the dark?

Is he lost forever?

Suddenly I *smell* him!

"There you are, my stinky little Nebit. Hurray!
Let's go home – and I'll hold your lead tight
this time!"

Woof!

Finding Nebit

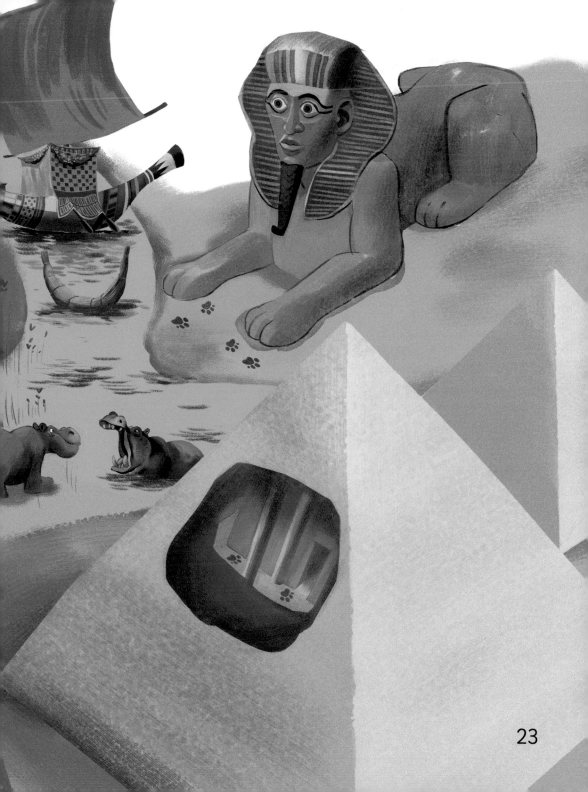

After reading

Letters and Sounds: Phase 5
Word count: 295
Focus phonemes: /f/ ph, /w/ wh, /ee/ e-e, e, y, /igh/ y, /ch/ tch, /j/ g, ge, dge, /l/ le, /z/ se, /sh/ ch, /ai/ a
Common exception words: of, to, the, into, are, one, oh, their, friend
Curriculum links: History
National Curriculum learning objectives: Spoken language: articulate and justify answers, arguments and opinions; Reading/Word reading: apply phonic knowledge and skills as the route to decode words, read accurately by blending sounds in unfamiliar words containing GPCs that have been taught, read words with contractions and understand that the apostrophe represents the omitted letter(s), read aloud accurately books that are consistent with their developing phonic knowledge; Reading/Comprehension: understand both the books they can already read accurately and fluently ... by: predicting what might happen on the basis of what has been read so far

Developing fluency

- The child may enjoy hearing you read the book. Model reading with lots of expression. Model reading those sentences with ellipses (three dots) – draw attention to the ellipses and model pausing to build tension.
- You may wish to take it in turns to read a page.

Phonic practice

- Talk about how the same sound can be written in different ways. For example, the /j/ sound in the following words:
  barge   nudge   giant
- Ask your child to sound out and blend each word:
  b/ar/ge   n/u/dge   g/i/a/n/t
- Talk about the different ways that the /j/ sound is spelled in these words.
- Can your child think of any other words that contain the /j/ sound? (e.g. *fudge, ginger, large*)

Extending vocabulary

- Flick through the book together and look for words that describe how Nebit moves throughout the story. (runs, scurries, scuttles, sprints, bounds, leaps)
- Ask your child:
  o Which of these words do you think work particularly well in describing how Nebit moves? Why?